Tricycle

Groundwood Books / House of Anansi Press
110 Spadina Avenue, Suite 801, Toronto, Ontario M5V 2K4
Distributed in the USA by Publishers Group West
1700 Fourth Street, Berkeley, CA 94710

We acknowledge for their financial support of our publishing program the Canada Council for the Arts,
the Government of Canada through the Book Publishing Industry Development Program (BPIDP) and
the Ontario Arts Council.

ONTARIO ARTS COUNCIL
CONSEIL DES ARTS DE L'ONTARIO

Library and Archives Canada Cataloging in Publication
Amado, Elisa
Tricycle / by Elisa Amado ; pictures by Alfonso Ruano.
ISBN-13: 978-0-88899-614-5
ISBN-10: 0-88899-614-4
I. Ruano, Alfonso II. Title.
PS8551.M335T75 2007   jC813'.6   C2006-904935-1

The illustrations are in acrylic.
Designed by Alfonso Ruano
Printed and bound in China

Tricycle

Elisa Amado   Alfonso Ruano

GROUNDWOOD BOOKS
HOUSE OF ANANSI PRESS
TORONTO   BERKELEY

I walk outside in my bare feet. The grass is wet and spiky but my feet don't hurt.

They are hard on the bottom because I never wear shoes unless I have to.

I run over to the pine tree and climb up the trunk until I reach my favorite branch. There is a little spot of gum from the tree on my blouse. It won't come off when it is washed so I will probably have a stain on my blouse forever, but I don't care. I climb higher until I can see over the hedge.

8

On one side of the hedge is my garden.
Clementina, my dog, is lying in the grass.
Timoteo is digging in the flower bed.
Sometimes I stay beside him while he works
and play with my cars. When he waters the
flowers the water runs into the little ditches I
dig and makes rivers for the cars to cross.

9

As I watch, Timoteo walks over to Clementina and scratches her stomach.

Her leg makes a funny scratching motion in the air every time he tickles her.

Timoteo laughs and goes back to work.

11

On the other side of the hedge are the shacks where Rosario, Chepe and Juanita live. I can see their mother making tortillas in the doorway. We buy her tortillas for lunch every day.

Right below the tree is a hole in the hedge where I like to hide.

Yesterday I left my tricycle down there when my mother called me and

told me to come in.

Climbing into the hedge is very prickly. It smells dusty and the air is kind of thick and dark. But no one can see me. Sometimes Rosario climbs in from the other side and hides with me.

Up in my tree I can feel the north wind blowing and it is a little bit cold. But the air is so clear I can see the smoke billowing away from the top of the Volcán de Fuego. It is always erupting. That is why it is called Fire. I wonder if Fuego could explode on us. I hope fire doesn't fall on us from the sky.

I hear Chepe's voice and look down.

Someone is crawling into the hedge.

I watch. Then I see someone poking through

on my side.

My tricycle is disappearing into the hedge. I watch and watch, and I hear whispers. Then I see Rosario and her brother, Chepe, crawling out of the other side pulling my tricycle. Their mother isn't in the doorway anymore. They push my tricycle over to their house and hide it under a box that is lying in the yard. My stomach feels funny. I don't say anything. My mother always tells me not to leave my toys outside.

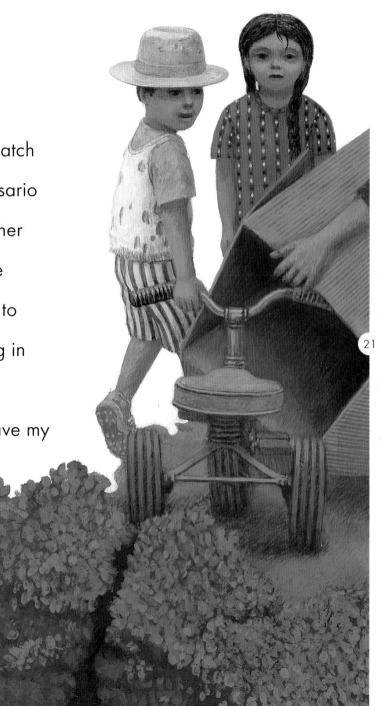

"Margarita, Margarita!" My mother is calling me to say that it is time for lunch. I climb down as fast as I can and run into the house. "Where's your trike?" she scolds.

"I don't know," I say.

There are guests for lunch. I am not listening to them. Instead I am making a little river in my potatoes with the gravy. I wish I could go outside again. But then I hear the word "tricycle." I see that Señora Alejos is talking. I hear her say, "They're all thieves. They should be shot."

I jump up and run to my bedroom. I crawl under the bed and lie there waiting for footsteps to come. But they don't and I fall asleep. When I wake up there is a little plate with green grapes on it on the floor by the bed. I eat them one by one.

When I walk into the library where my mother is reading a book, she looks up at me.

"My tricycle got run over by a big black car," I say. "Then some men with guns took it away with them. They almost ran over Clementina. I don't care because I'm too old for a trike now, anyway."

I climb into my mother's lap and she gives me a hug. "Don't worry," she says. "No one is going to get shot."

I look around the room. I can smell my mother's perfume. I feel safe.

"I hope Fuego doesn't erupt on us," I say. "Our house is strong but Rosario's house could get all burned up."

I jump off her lap and go outside. I don't think I feel like climbing the tree, so I go over and watch Timoteo plant some flowers.